KING ARTHUR
AND THE KNIGHTS
OF THE ROUND TABLE

by M. C. Hall

illustrated by C. E. Richards

LIBRARIAN REVIEWER
Allyson A.W. Lyga MS - Library Media/Graphic Novel Consultant
Fulbright Memorial Fund Scholar, author

READING CONSULTANT
Mark DeYoung - Classroom Teacher, Edina Public Schools, Minnesota
BA in Elementary Education, Central College
MS in Curriculum & Instruction, University of Minnesota

Graphic Revolve is published by Stone Arch Books
151 Good Counsel Drive, P.O. Box 669
Mankato, Minnesota 56002
www.stonearchbooks.com

Library of Congress Cataloging-in-Publication Data
Hall, Margaret, 1947–
    King Arthur and the Knights of the Round Table/ retold by M. C. Hall; illustrated
by C. E. Richards.
    p. cm.—(Graphic Revolve)
    ISBN-13: 978-1-59889-048-8 (library binding)
    ISBN-10: 1-59889-048-4 (library binding)
    ISBN-13: 978-1-59889-218-5 (paperback)
    ISBN-10: 1-59889-218-5 (paperback)
    1. Graphic novels. I. Richards, C. E. II. Title. III. Series.
PN6727.H255K56 2007
741.5'973—dc22   2006007693

Summary: In a world of wizards, giants, and dragons, King Arthur and the Knights of
the Round Table are the only defense against the forces of evil that threaten the kingdom
of Camelot.

Credits
Art Director: Heather Kindseth
Cover Graphic Designer: Heather Kindseth and Kay Fraser
Interior Graphic Designer: Heather Kindseth

1 2 3 4 5 6 11 10 09 08 07 06

Printed in the China

TABLE OF CONTENTS

KING ARTHUR

LANCELOT

GUINEVERE

MERLIN

GALAHAD

MORDRED

CHAPTER 1

Long ago, in a dark time, two mighty armies fought.

Uther Pendragon, king of Britain, fought Gorlois, the duke of Cornwall. Uther wanted to marry the duke's beautiful wife, Igraine.

I would give anything to beat my enemy.

Anything, my lord?

Uther Pendragon won the battle. Gorlois was killed, and Igraine became the new queen of Britain.

Nine months later, a child's cry is heard through the darkness.

And in the darkness, Uther's promise is remembered.

In another part of the great city . . .

The holiday was also a time for games. Sir Ector and his son, Sir Kay, headed toward the jousting fields. With them was Kay's younger brother, Arthur.

Look at the crowds, father!

A fine knight I am! I've forgotten my sword!

I'll find one, brother!

Where will I find a sword for Kay?

Arthur ran through the dark streets.

I know! I saw a sword in the town square!

Arthur was in too much of a hurry to read the words on the stone.

Arthur got into the Lady's boat. It took him to the center of the lake.

The boat carried Arthur back to shore. By then, the Lady of the Lake was gone.

Excalibur is mine!

Several days later . . .

Guinevere, the most beautiful woman in the world!

I have brought peace to Britain, Merlin. Shouldn't I marry now?

Is there a lady you fancy?

She is indeed beautiful. Yet I wish you wanted someone else.

She is all I could hope for.

I can see your future, Arthur. This princess shall bring about the end of your kingdom.

But I can also see your heart. You truly wish for her.

Good wizard, speak to her father for me.

As you command, my king.

At the castle of King Leodegrance . . .

King Arthur asks to marry your daughter, sire.

He is a noble king. My land shall be his, as shall my knights.

And your daughter?

I share my father's high opinion of Arthur. I shall be honored to be his queen.

A wedding date was set.

Guinevere's father sent a huge round table as a wedding gift.

Since this table has no head or foot, every knight is equal.

But why is that seat empty?

I shall sit here!

NOOOOOO!!!!

What's happening?

AHH!

An eager young knight reached for the mysterious chair . . .

The poor knight's skeleton crashed to the floor.

ROAAAR!

ZZAK!

I owe you my life, sir knight!

Lancelot returned Elaine to her father's castle.

Welcome. I am King Pelles. For freeing my daughter, Elaine, you shall always have my sword whenever you need it.

King Pelles celebrated Lancelot's brave rescue of Elaine.

But the king also had plans for the noble knight and his lovely daughter.

Lancelot shall soon drink the potion. The prophecy shall come true.

A witch had shown King Pelles a strange vision. Whoever would bear Lancelot's child would give birth to the greatest knight in the world.

Lancelot realized he had been tricked by Pelles and his daughter.

He also knew Guinevere would be angry to hear he was wed, because she loved him.

He felt ashamed. So he rode off into a deep forest, far away from Camelot.

In good time, Elaine's son was born. She named him Galahad and raised him in a faraway castle among wise men and women.

Many years passed. Lancelot became a wild knight of the woods.

Arthur's knights passed through many adventures as they searched for the Holy Grail.

Finally, three of Arthur's knights — Galahad, Percival, and Bors — came to a ruined castle.

Look! It is Lancelot.

Galahad drank from the cup, and then . . .

Galahad and the Grail were never seen again.

His fellow knights returned to Camelot without him.

Soon the whispers reached Arthur. He had no choice but to send Guinevere away.

When Lancelot heard the news, he left Camelot as well.

Arthur was alone. And Mordred continued to plot in the shadows.

Arthur is weak. Join me, and we will rule Britain.

The price of battle was high.

That night, Arthur dreamed . . .

Merlin, Merlin, where are you?

It was not Merlin, but Galahad who appeared in a vision.

Do not fight this day, Arthur. Make peace with Mordred. In a month, Lancelot will come to help you.

Suddenly, Arthur awoke.

The next morning, Arthur made his plans.

Take this to Mordred. Offer him a portion of my land. We must have peace.

Yes, my lord.

The two sides prepared to meet.

If anyone draws his sword, kill Mordred at once. I do not trust him.

If anyone draws his sword, kill them all!

By dark, the field was covered with bodies.

My noble knights! So many lost!

At the same time, inside Arthur's castle . . .

The Round Table!

It is splitting apart!

From his vantage point, Arthur saw Mordred.

Traitor! You shall pay!

ABOUT SIR THOMAS MALORY

The story of King Arthur is an ancient legend that storytellers passed down for many generations. The story was first told sometime before the 11th century. Finally, in the 15th century, Sir Thomas Malory wrote down his version of these stories. He titled the collection *The Book of King Arthur and His Noble Knights of the Round Table*.

People know little about Malory's interest in the stories of King Arthur. He likely heard different versions of these stories when he was growing up. Perhaps his life experience as a knight helped him better understand the good and evil forces in the King Arthur stories.

ABOUT THE AUTHOR

M. C. Hall has written more than 80 fiction and nonfiction books for children, including science books, biographies, and fairy tales. She likes to read, walk on the beach, garden, and ski. She lives in the Boston area.

ABOUT THE ILLUSTRATOR

C. E. Richards grew up reading comic books, C. S. Lewis, J. R. R. Tolkien, and watching *Star Wars*. He is a graduate of Savannah College of Art and lives in Atlanta, where he is working on book and magazine illustrations, comic books, poster design, playbill illustration, and album artwork for CDs.

GLOSSARY

archbishop (arch-BISH-up)—the ruler of bishops in some Christian religions

duke (DOOK)—in Britain, a person ranked lower than a prince

fortress (FOR-truhss)—a group of buildings protected by walls and forts

hermit (HUR-mit)—a person who lives alone and away from others

joust (JOWST)—a battle with lances or spears fought between knights on horseback

moat (MOHT)—a deep, wide ditch filled with water that surrounds a castle or fortress and keeps people away

perilous (PARE-uhl-uhss)—dangerous

potion (PO-shuhn)—a drink with special powers

prophesy (PROF-uh-see)—a prediction

rebel (REB-uhl)—a person who doesn't follow rules

scabbard (SKAB-urd)—a case that people wear to hold a sword

wizard (WIZ-urd)—a person with magical powers

BACKGROUND ON THE KNIGHTS OF THE ROUND TABLE

The stories of King Arthur and the Knights of the Round Table take place in Britain during the Middle Ages, a time period that lasted from the 5th to the 15th century A.D. This was a period of unrest in Britain and Europe as people fought many wars for control of the land. Britain wasn't a united country at the time.
Kings and lords throughout what is now England, Wales, and Scotland ruled over small regions scattered across the countryside.

Many people wonder if the legends of King Arthur are real and if the places in the story really existed. Some historians believe that the castle Camelot and the island of Avalon are based on real places in England. For example, some people believe that Arthur is buried beneath the town of Glastonbury. Visitors still travel to England to retrace the steps of King Arthur and his knights.

KING ARTHUR'S BRITAIN

N

W   **E**

S

🏰 POSSIBLE
LOCATIONS
OF CAMELOT

SCOTLAND

ENGLAND

WALES

London •

*(legendary
burial site of
King Arthur)*

Glastonbury
✕

Atlantic Ocean

*English
Channel*

DISCUSSION QUESTIONS

1. Why did the Round Table break into two pieces?

2. At the end of the story, we find out that King Arthur and the Knights of the Round Table will return someday. Name some times when you could use the help of Arthur and the knights.

3. Would you like to go back to the times of King Arthur? Why or why not?

4. When Arthur was a boy, how did people know that he was really the king?

WRITING PROMPTS

1. Imagine that you were given the sword Excalibur. Explain what you would do with its magical powers. (Remember, the sword can only be used for good.)

2. Describe your favorite character in the story. Is it Arthur or Guinevere? Lancelot or Merlin? What does your favorite character look like? Why do you like this character the best?

3. The Knights of the Round Table go on a quest to find the Holy Grail. Their journey took a long time. Write about a quest, or journey, that you went on. What did you find at the end of it?

OTHER BOOKS

The Adventures of Tom Sawyer

Tom Sawyer is the cleverest of characters, constantly outwitting those around him. Then there is Huckleberry Finn, the envy of the town's schoolchildren because he has the rare gift of complete freedom, never attending school or answering to anyone but himself. After Tom and Huck witness a murder, they find themselves on a series of adventures that lead them to some seriously frightening situations.

The Hunchback of Notre Dame

Hidden away in the bell tower of the Cathedral of Notre Dame, Quasimodo is treated like a beast. Although he is gentle and kind, he has the reputation of a frightening monster because of his physical deformities. He develops affection for Esmeralda, a gypsy girl who shows him kindness in return. When the girl is sentenced to an unfair death by hanging, Quasimodo is determined to save her. But those closest to Quasimodo have other plans for the gypsy.